Rarity
✦✦✦ and ✦✦✦
The Curious
Case of Charity

Written by G. M. Berrow

Little, Brown and Company
New York ✶ Boston

Little, Brown and Company

Hachette Book Group
237 Park Avenue, New York, NY 10017
Visit our website at lb-kids.com

Little, Brown and Company is a division of Hachette Book Group, Inc.
The Little, Brown name and logo are trademarks of Hachette Book Group, Inc.

The publisher is not responsible for websites (or their content) that are not owned by the publisher.

First Edition: April 2014

Library of Congress Cataloging-in-Publication Data

Berrow, G. M.
    Rarity and the curious case of Charity / written by G. M. Berrow. — First edition.
        pages cm. — (My little pony)
    Summary: "Rarity is excited to welcome her new apprentice, Charity, to Ponyville. Rarity is sure that the two of them will become best friends, bonding over their love of fashion and glamour. But after Charity dyes her mane and tail to look more like her mentor, and begins to copy the fashionista's every move, Rarity realizes this pony is a problem!"— Provided by publisher.
    ISBN 978-0-316-24808-2 (pbk.) — ISBN 978-0-316-32091-7 (ebook)
    I. Title.
    PZ7.B4615Rar 2014
    [Fic]—dc23

                                                                    2013034583

10 9 8 7 6 5 4 3 2

RRD-C

Printed in the United States of America

For Kiki—and all
those who embody
the Element of
generosity

CONTENTS

✴ ✴ ✴

CHAPTER 1

A Pony of Prominence

✦ ✦ ✦

The mail in Equestria could be unreliable, but the Ponyville Post had an especially poor reputation for punctuality. In fact, it was one of the slowest post office branches around. It didn't matter what sort of parcel a pony was sending: It could be a birthday card to a friend, a thank-you note to the host of a fabulous event in Canterlot, or even a shipment of silky skirts to a boutique in Neigh Mexicolt, and it would take ages.

But even though she was well aware of its slowpoke track record, Rarity couldn't understand why she still hadn't received *the* letter yet: the letter that would solidify her status as a pony of prominence in modern Equestrian fashion.

It just didn't make a stitch of sense! Rarity had applied to the House of Outrageous and Opulent Fashion (H.O.O.F.) Summer Mentor Program months ago and still hadn't heard a peep. At the time, she had been positive she was going to be accepted as a mentor. Why wouldn't they want a pony like her? Rarity had designed for princesses, pop stars, and the Canterlot elite! Why, there was nopony more perfectly suited to guide a young, impressionable designer through the world of fashion and fabulosity. At the very least, she could teach a young pony how to achieve the perfect mane curl, she thought as she inspected her own purple locks in the mirror.

Rarity trotted over to steal a glance out the front window of the Carousel Boutique. She imagined that she was the main character in a storybook called *Raponyzel*. She was a forlorn damsel locked in a tower, with only her flowing, spectacular mane for company. Rarity wasn't trapped in the Carousel Boutique, but she did feel hopeless just like the story's heroine. Where was her letter?

The mailbox out front was adorned with glittering yellow gems. It was really quite pretty. As beautiful as something could look on the outside, Rarity still believed that what was on the inside counted more—especially in this case. Would it be another empty mailbox day, or would her precious, fate-altering letter be there?

There was no way to know for sure, but Rarity had a dreadful feeling about it. Just *dreadful*. She probably shouldn't even bother going outside and checking. She should probably just stay inside and work. She trudged down the stairs as if she were headed back to the mines.

She was lucky that the boutique doubled as her home and as her shop—an inviting retreat filled with treasures. The clothes on the racks were all beautiful, and all designed exclusively by her. She spent both her days and her nights dreaming up wares that were "chic, unique, and *magnifique*."

"Sweetie Belle?" she called out to her little sister. The young filly was probably down in the workroom pawing through the fabrics again. She had recently requested that her sister make her some new curtains for her clubhouse and was desperate for the perfect pattern.

Sweetie Belle appeared in the doorway, eyes wide and hopeful. "What's up, Rarity?"

"Would you be a dear and go check? I simply *cannot* face the disappointment again." Then Rarity sighed dramatically and collapsed onto a red velvet sofa. It just happened to be situated in the perfect position for her to gracefully swoon.

"I have so much to do already, anyway. This order of performance dresses for the Ponyville Choir is plenty more work than I thought it would be. Fifteen dresses and bow ties for the stallions, too! What in Equestria was I thinking?!" At least the Pony Tones, the other musical act in town, had only four members.

If only Rarity had a little helping hoof of an apprentice, everything would go much faster. But even so, she would never admit to the other ponies that she wasn't able to maintain a shop on her own. Even when she was stressed out, Rarity thought it was important to keep up a certain elegant image. One of her favorite French designers, Coco Cheval, used to say, "A mare should be two things: classy and fabulous." Rarity liked to think she embodied each at all times.

"Rarity!" Sweetie Belle's little shouts came in through the window. "Rarity! Come out here!"

Rarity perked up. Could it be? Was *the*

letter finally here? Thank Celestia, she could relax and start to prepare for her role as a fabulous, yet sage mentor. *My goodness,* she thought. *What does a mentor wear? Some sort of robe? An elaborate hat?* There were a lot of directions she could take this thing in, fashion-wise.

"Rarity!" Sweetie Belle called out again.

Oh right, Rarity thought. Better check that she was even in the program first. Rarity smoothed down her violet mane and trotted outside to join her sister. Her heart began to beat a little bit faster.

CHAPTER 2

good News from Manehattan

✦ ✦ ✦

Rarity was surprised to see that the little pink-and-lavender-maned filly wasn't
holding anything in her hoof. "Well,
where is it?!" Rarity shrieked, then stopped
herself. Raising one's voice was not very
refined. "*Ahem.* I mean...I thought you

said it was here." She motioned to the mailbox.

"No, I called you out here because I can't reach the back!" Sweetie Belle's tiny voice cracked as she explained. "I think there's something in there, but I'm too short." The little filly looked down at the ground in defeat. "Which just proves that I'm a blank flank *and* a shorty!"

It was true.

"That isn't true!" comforted Rarity.

For all their trying, Sweetie Belle and her two best friends, Scootaloo and Apple Bloom, *still* hadn't earned their cutie marks. "It's the worst. Possible. Thing!" Sweetie Belle cried out, and pretended to faint on the front lawn. Rarity smirked. Her little sister was certainly learning a thing or two about drama. Sometimes, Rarity couldn't believe how much Sweetie Belle learned from her. It was cute.

"Calm down, Sweetie," Rarity tutted. "You know that you'll earn your cutie mark when it's the right time. Now, what do we have here?" Rarity reached inside the mailbox and pulled out...a letter!

The envelope was gray, edged in silver, and addressed to *Miss Rarity, Carousel Boutique, Ponyville, Equestria.* This was definitely it. Rarity's eyes sparkled with the same excitement as when she found a rare gem with her Unicorn magic. She wanted to rip it open, but she chose to display restraint and poise.

Rarity gently lifted the flap of the envelope with her magic and lifted out its contents.

YOU'RE INVITED!
TO A BIRTHDAY PARTY
AT THE ROCK FARM
FOR
CLOUDY QUARTZ

*Please, oh please RSVP and come
and be our guest!*

The last part was scribbled in Pinkie's hoofwriting. Real gravel, presumably from the rock farm, was glued around the edges as decoration. A few tiny bits of sandstone fell to the ground like sad confetti, and Rarity shoved the invitation back inside the envelope. She didn't bother to read the rest of the invitation. "Well, that's a rocky road," she said, slumping down.

It wasn't that she didn't want to go to the party. It was just that getting the invite now instead of what she had been expecting made Rarity feel tricked. It was almost like the time she had ordered a bolt of cerulean-blue satin and accidentally received lime-green charmeuse instead. There was nothing really wrong with the lime fabric—it just wasn't what she *wanted*. What she needed now was a H.O.O.F. acceptance letter.

"What's wrong, Rarity?" Sweetie Belle looked very concerned. "Did H.O.O.F. reject you from the thingy? Do you want me to make you something to eat to help you feel better?" It was sweet of her to offer, but Sweetie Belle didn't have the best track record with cooking. She had once even managed to burn a glass of orange juice, along with the toast and eggs that were supposed to go with it.

Rarity shook her head in protest. "No, no, no. Nothing awful like *that*. It's just—" But before she could finish her sentence, a blur of gray and yellow zipped past them and smashed right into the side of the Carousel Boutique. *CRASH!*

A moment later, the mail pony—a gray Pegasus with a yellow mane—got up and came trotting over to them. She still looked a little dizzy from her awkward landing, and she was a bit dirty. But it didn't matter... because she was holding a purple envelope in her mouth! It had to be it.

"Mmmmf umph mrrfff, ump mrfffn

ferf," the mail pony mumbled to the Unicorn sisters. Then she bowed her head to them, dropped the envelope, and took off into the sky. The Pegasus was still a bit shaky as she flew in a zigzag pattern rather than a straight line. How utterly odd that pony could be sometimes. What was her name again? Rarity tried to recall it, but she never could remember.

"Excuse *moi*?" Rarity called out to the sky. "Miss mail pony! What was that you said again, daaaaarling?"

"She said sorry for losing the letter at the Ponyville Post, but she found it again and it's for you," Sweetie Belle explained with a shrug.

"I'm not going to even ask how you understood that," Rarity commented. "The important thing is—it's here!" Rarity let out a little squeal of satisfied delight. She inspected the golden seal on the envelope and immediately recognized the H.O.O.F. crest. It was a coat of legs—a little shield pattern divided into four sections. Each portion bore a different fashion item: a fabulous shoe, a grand hat, a glittering necklace, and an exquisite dress. All of Rarity's favorite things.

" 'To the illustrious Rarity of Ponyville,' " she read aloud from the paper. " 'We are honored to welcome you to one of the most exclusive and prestigious societies in Equestrian fashion today—the H.O.O.F. Mentors!' "

"Yay!" Sweetie Belle jumped up and down.

" 'We have taken great care to assign you an apprentice who we feel will benefit from your guidance. You will soon be

joined by Sweetmint, a student from Larsons The Neigh School for Design and—'"
Rarity mumbled the rest as she scanned the page. Suddenly, the smile fell from her face. "Oh no!"

"What?!" Sweetie Belle craned to see the letter. "What is it, Rarity?"

"This is a disaster! How will I ever be ready in time?" Rarity put her hoof to her chest in exasperation. "She arrives... *tomorrow!*"

CHAPTER 3

Welcome to Ponyville

✴ ✴ ✴

Rarity was so lucky that her five best friends had offered to go with her to the train station. It was like the new apprentice's own little welcoming committee. Pinkie Pie, Applejack, Fluttershy, Princess Twilight Sparkle, and Rainbow Dash always made things extra special. Rarity knew because having them around made her shine a little brighter—like a recently polished gem. It just proved that the enhanced sheen of one's coat could be counted among friendship's many benefits.

"This is so exciting, Rarity!" said Twilight Sparkle, trying to catch up to her. "Your very own student." Her eyes were alight with an excitement only brought on by academia. Twilight loved everything associated with learning. "I'd love to have a student of my own someday!"

"Does sound kinda nice," Applejack chimed in. "Sometimes I think I could use a little more help around the farm. Other than Apple Bloom and Big Mac, of course." She tipped her yellow cowgirl hat. "Not that they don't do a mighty fine job."

"Well, I'm not hosting her because I

need *help*," Rarity explained defensively. "It's more of a 'giving back to Equestria' sort of endeavor."

Applejack glanced at her sideways. "How do you figure that?"

"I am going to guide an up-and-comer through the daunting, yet rewarding industry of fashion, of course. It's the least that I can do to give back to the community that *made* me." She puffed up with pride.

"Having an intern to boss around seems pretty cool," said Rainbow Dash, hovering above them long enough to give her two bits. "If *I* had a rookie Pegasus to do whatever I wanted her to, I'd make her do all the boring stuff for me so I could fly all day!" she shouted, taking off into the distance and leaving a rainbow trail behind her.

"*Apprentice*, not intern," Rarity corrected,

picking up her pace even more. "Now hurry along!" It would be awful if this poor, confused Sweetmint was standing on the empty train platform alone. What would that say about Rarity's attitudes toward punctuality? It was imperative to set a good example from now on.

"Well, whatever you want to call her—I'm very proud of you. Being a teacher is such a rewarding experience," Twilight Sparkle added. "Or so I'm learning from all those little fillies I've been helping out at the Golden Oak Library lately. Maybe they're the ones who are actually teaching me!" Twilight laughed at her joke. "So, have you made any lesson plans yet? If you need some ideas, I have some great guides that—"

"Thank you, dear," Rarity answered

quickly. There was no telling how long Twilight would ramble about schoolwork if given the chance.

Rarity scanned the way ahead. Was that the Friendship Express chugging into the station already? She thought she could make out little puffs of white smoke in the sky. "*Tout de suite*, girls! I think the train has already arrived!" She pranced ahead frantically.

The ponies tried to go as fast as they could. Twilight cantered alongside Applejack on the ground, the pair leaving little puffs of dirt in their wake. Fluttershy tried to fly fast, but because her wingbeats were so gentle, she barely rustled up a breeze. Pinkie Pie bounded forward with a smile on her face. She always bounced as if there were springs on her hooves. And Rainbow Dash was…already at the station. But she was the fastest Pegasus in Ponyville, so that was no major surprise to anypony.

"See, guys? Ten seconds flat!" Rainbow Dash bragged through a cheesy grin when the others finally caught up. She wasn't a very modest pony. "About time you slowponies got here."

"Speaking of *flat*." Rarity gasped, catching her own reflection in the glass window of the station. "Look at my mane! It looks hideous! Where is the curl? Where is the *bounce*? Where is the body?"

"And this!" she cried, noticing a chip in her hooficure polish. What a state she was in. She hoped that Sweetmint wouldn't take notice of that, either. It would be terrible to shatter the illusion of perfection she'd worked so hard to achieve. Even though nopony was perfect, Rarity liked to think she often came close. At least, she tried to. "Well, there goes making a good first impression on my young protégé."

"Well, I think ya look great, Rarity!" assured Applejack. The others nodded in agreement.

"She's totally right! As right as . . . chocolate rain!" said Pinkie Pie, licking her lips. "Mmmmm, chocolate rain. I miss it so much. . . ." Pinkie looked to the sky in mock despair. "We haven't had any in for*EVER*!"

"That's because Discord is a good little draconequus now and isn't causing any trouble," said Fluttershy in her soft voice. She smiled sweetly. "But I bet if you asked him as a *friend*, he might do you a favor. . . ."

"A flavor?!" Pinkie's eyes grew wide just thinking of all the scrumptious possibilities. "Like, any flavor rain I want?"

Fluttershy shook her head in protest. "No, no, I said a *fav*—"

Applejack held out her hoof to stop Fluttershy. "Don't bother, sugarcube. Just let her have this one." They watched as Pinkie rattled off a list of fantastical flavors. They couldn't help but giggle at her silliness.

Pinkie looked to the sky with a wide grin. "What about sprinkle–peanut butter–marshmallow-flavored rain? Or envelope-glue-taste rain? Or saltwater taffy! Pickle-barrel flavored? Kumquats! Oooooo... chimicherrychaaaaanga raaaain?!"

"Ponyville Station!" hollered the conductor stallion as the train doors opened with a hiss. A stream of exotic ponies began to exit the cars. Rarity was always on the lookout for inspiration in what others wore, so she was intrigued by the array of characters. She observed at least six different ponies sporting regional fashion trends, including a mare wearing her mane in the traditional Crystal Empire updo and a Unicorn filly wearing some Baltimare jelly hoof bracelets. Which would be her guest, though?

"So, do you know what she looks like?" asked Twilight, craning her neck for a better look at the crowd.

"I haven't the slightest idea," answered Rarity. "She could be that one in the hat there?" Rarity pointed her hoof at a tall, willowy pony with an aqua-colored coat. She was sporting an extravagant purple hat with feathers. Rarity shook her head. "But no, probably not." Feathers were very last year. Surely, her fashion apprentice would know better than to wear feathers!

Unless Rarity was out of the loop and feathers were back in style again? Rarity bit her lip in concern. The trends changed so fast, sometimes the second they reached Ponyville, they were out of style again in other cities.

"How will we know which one she is?" fretted Applejack, looking at the mass of ponies and scrunching her freckled nose. "It's like pickin' a horseshoe outta a haystack!"

"I think you mean a needle," teased Rainbow Dash. "A horseshoe in a haystack would be a cinch to find."

Applejack rolled her eyes. "Oh, apple-seeds, you knew what I meant!"

"Can you two please stop?" Rarity interrupted. "This is a crisis here!"

Applejack and Rainbow Dash exchanged a look. Rarity's idea of a crisis changed on a moment-by-moment basis.

"Just relax," Twilight assured. "We'll find her in no time."

"You're right." Rarity nodded and continued to scan the platform. "Maybe H.O.O.F. gave her a picture of me." Besides, Rarity figured, what sort of fashion pony in the know hadn't heard of her lately? She was the type of pony everypony should know. Especially a pony who was part of the H.O.O.F. program.

At the very least, Sweetmint must have heard of the Carousel Boutique. It was practically synonymous with luxury these days. The society pages of the local newspapers were littered with pictures of elite ponies wearing Rarity's fashions. She'd received orders from all over, which meant that her designs were definitely making appearances in all the elite social circles across Equestria.

"Whoa, who's that?" Spike said, eyes growing wide. He pointed his little dragon claw in the direction of a young Unicorn. She had a white coat, light green mane and tail, and a cutie mark of three light blue, heart-shaped gems. She wore a dark green, rhinestone-studded scarf that was expertly draped around her pretty neck. She was turning her head left to right, clearly looking for somepony in particular. She wore the "hopelessly lost" look well.

It had to be her.

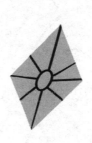

CHAPTER 4

City Pony

★ ★ ★

"That's her!" exclaimed Rarity as she pranced off toward the newcomer. The others followed her lead.

"Isn't she a student?" asked Twilight Sparkle. "Where are her books?"

"Maybe she packed them." Fluttershy

shrugged. The pony did have several suit-cases stacked high next to her.

"You must be Sweetmint from Manehat-tan," said Rarity, smiling as she approached the lost soul. "Welcome to Ponyville!"

"Yes!" The Unicorn breathed a sigh of relief, then squealed, "That's me!" She was practically exploding with excitement upon seeing her mentor. "Oh, Rarity! Wow! It's, like . . . *really* you!" Her big golden eyes wid-ened. "But how did you know what I looked like?" Sweetmint's face was that of a pony who had just seen somepony like Sapphire Shores or Trenderhoof trot by—filled with complete adoration and starstruck awe. Rarity liked that about her.

"Oh, *I didn't*." Rarity walked around the new pony, sizing her up. "But I spied your utterly fabulous look and thought: *Only a true fashionista like myself would know that forest green is* the *color of the moment!* Tell me—is the scarf one of your own designs?" This mentor thing was going even better than she anticipated. Rarity could already tell that Sweetmint was a pony after her own heart. "Oh, it's such an absolute pleasure to meet you, darling."

Sweetmint's sleek, pale green mane swayed gently from side to side as she shook her head in disbelief. "I can't believe it's actually you! I'm such a big fan of your work. You, like... totally look even *more* amazing in pony than you do in pictures. I got this one out of *Mare Éclair.*" She riffled through her saddlebag, procured a rumpled magazine clipping, and held it out for everypony to see. It was a photo of Rarity from Princess Cadance and Shining Armor's royal wedding, along with a feature article about her—the pony who had designed the bridle gown. A few more clippings fell to the ground, and Sweetmint scrambled to pick them up.

"That little blurb? *Stop*, darling!" Rarity flipped her mane and laughed. "No, no, please continue if you must, Sweetmint."

"Actually, my name is Charity," the Unicorn admitted. At this, her eyes began to dart around nervously. "I, uh…don't know why H.O.O.F. put my, uh…my *nickname* down. Just, um, Charity."

"Oh, well, all right, then, *Charity*," said Rarity, raising a suspicious eyebrow. She wasn't sure why the sudden name switch bothered her. Maybe she just felt a little silly to have been calling her the wrong thing this entire time. Yes, that was it.

Pinkie Pie popped her head in between them and stage-whispered, "Wooooo, that's super-duper spooky-tastical. Your names are almost...the same name."

"Rarity and *Charity*," Applejack marveled. "Well, what d'ya know?"

Fluttershy smiled. "That's nice."

"Interesting..." Rainbow Dash was unconvinced. She crossed her arms and looked Charity up and down. "Your name's really Charity?"

"Mmmhmm," Charity replied, looking at the other ponies curiously. "What's yours?"

Rarity put her hoof to her forehead. "Silly me! I didn't even introduce you." Rarity pointed at the group. "This is Rainbow Dash, Applejack, Fluttershy, Pinkie Pie, and...her Grand Royal Majesty Princess

Twilight Sparkle." Rarity put a flourish on the last part. She was very proud of being best friends with royalty—and with the rest of them, too, of course. "My very best friends in the whole world."

"Rarity's friends! Princess!" Charity bowed her head at the ponies. "What an honor! I still can't believe I'm here with Rarity and now I'm hanging out with all of you, too." She looked to each of them with a huge smile. "This is so unreal. In a good way."

"Shall we?" Rarity motioned her hoof toward the exit.

Charity started to pick up her things, but Rarity stopped her. "Spike will take care of your luggage."

"Wow, thanks!" Charity beamed. Her big eyes sparkled, framed by dark eyelashes. Rarity wondered if they were natural or if the young pony had to use false ones like she did.

"Spiiiike?" Rarity singsonged again. She wasn't accustomed to being ignored, especially by her biggest fan. "The luggage, please?"

But Spike didn't respond in his usual prompt manner. He just stood still. The baby dragon was completely mesmerized. The ponies had only ever seen him making those heart-shaped eyes toward one other pony before—Rarity herself. The one pony he had had a not-so-secret crush on for basically forever.

"Don't worry, Rarity," said Twilight Sparkle, nudging past the distracted dragon. She trotted over to the stack of bags. "We'll help. Right, girls?"

"Darn tootin'!" Applejack nodded and

trotted over to pick up a large green case with yellow daisies patterned all over it. Pinkie Pie bounced after her and shouted, "I'll take the pink one!"

"No, wait!" shouted Spike, snapping out of his daze. "I'll take one!" He scrambled to grab the biggest case—a brown one with stickers all over it from different places in Equestria. He made a big show of it.

Charity giggled. "Thank you, sir."

"At your service, miss." Spike bowed. "It's my pleasure."

Charity's expression turned to one of concern. She lowered her voice and whispered to Rarity, "I sure hope everypony likes me."

"Don't worry, dear," Rarity assured the new girl. She trotted to her side, put a hoof around her, and started to lead her out of the station. "If you're anything like me, we'll all become fast friends!"

"But I can guarantee I'll be the fastest!" Rainbow Dash shouted as she shot off into the distance, leaving a bright rainbow trailing behind her.

Charity looked to Rarity in awe. "This is all so brilliant!"

"If you're impressed already"—Rarity flipped her mane—"just wait 'til you see my boutique."

CHAPTER 5

Tea for Two

★ ★ ★

Fweeeee! The teakettle whistled and a gust
of steam shot out. Rarity used her horn to
magic her prettiest tea set out of the cup-
board. The cups were white with gold-
plated rims and handles, and the saucers
were plum colored and encrusted with rare
violet gemstones. She only used the set on

very special occasions. Either when she was stuck on a project and needed a little pick-me-up, or when she had a guest over who was worthy of the very best. As it happened, Charity was a very special guest at the Carousel Boutique. She deserved special treatment.

"I can't tell you how *thrilled* I am to have somepony around who appreciates style just as much as I do," Rarity said, pouring the hot water from the gilded teapot. Steam rose from the cup into delicious, fragrant swirls. It was lavender-and-Ceylon-flavored tea— Rarity's favorite. It would go perfectly with the Bluedazzle berry tart that she had baked earlier.

"Ponyville is so quaint and adorable, but it doesn't have much of a fashion scene, you know? But of course, I do love it here even if it's no Manehattan. I could never be too far away from my friends. Are you originally from the city?"

"I'm actually from Fillydelphia! But I also studied abroad in Mare-is, Prance, last summer," Charity explained. "That was super cool."

"How divine!" Rarity gasped. "I would give anything to visit Prance! Are you a fan of Coco Cheval, too?"

"She's only my *idol*!" Charity squealed, standing up. "Other than you, Rarity."

"Now you're just flattering me." Rarity blushed. "Keep doing it if you must." Even though she'd only spent a few hours with Charity, it was safe to say that she would never tire of her compliments.

As Rarity continued preparing the tea, Charity looked around the boutique with fascination. "Wow! Now, this is a real designer's workshop. Not like mine back in my apartment in the city." The room was littered with half-unrolled bolts of fabric, pieces of patterns that had yet to be pinned, and glittery adornments of every shape and size. Straight pins stuck out of various cushions, and velvet ribbon clippings sat in neat piles underneath the sewing machine. The model ponnequins were outfitted in matching green dresses that were clearly some sort of work in progress. The forest green fabric was expertly draped and pinned but still far from completion.

"I told you the boutique was fabulous!" Rarity giggled.

"It is," Charity said dreamily. "I wish I owned one *just* like it."

It was so great to see that there were

ponies just like Rarity—ambitious and stylish. "Maybe someday you will!"

"A girl can dream." Charity skipped over to the half-clothed ponnequins. "Oh my giddy! What are these? The fabric is totally gorge! Very John Gallopiano. His spring line was awesome, right?" It was so lovely to talk to another pony about the world of fashion. Charity seemed to know her stuff.

"Those little things? They're hardly comparable to Gallopiano!" Rarity laughed. "They are a commission for the Ponyville Choir's Sweet Songs of Summer concert. But I'm afraid I absolutely detest what I've created thus far. If I had more time, I'd scrap these and start over completely." Rarity looked at the ponnequins wistfully. "Alas, every artist must go through their process."

"What's your process like?" The eager student leaned in closer. "Do you make pattern schematics or just raw sketches?"

"I do a little of everything. My process is always undergoing revisions." Part of Rarity's current process was denial. She had been doing a great job of ignoring the fact that she was on a deadline to finish the dresses. Charity's arrival had served as a wonderful distraction, but the Ponyville concert was next week! She really needed to finish sewing them. It would be terrible to disappoint Golden Harvest and the other singers who had practiced so hard.

Rarity had to be very careful these days after her disaster with Hoity Toity. The famous fashion critic had come to Ponyville to see the designs she'd created for her friends to wear to the Grand Galloping

Gala, but they were all tragically wrong. She'd taken too much advice from her clients, and the dresses had ended up as over-accessorized messes.

Now the choir dresses were in a similarly tragic state. They just looked like a mess of green satin with some ribbons hastily added as an afterthought. Not Carousel Boutique worthy at all. But she'd have plenty of time to sort them out later. Right now, her main priority was the new apprentice.

"Enough about me." Rarity sipped her tea. "I want to hear more about *you*, darling." She used her magic to dish up a piece of tart for her guest and took the seat across from her. "Bluedazzle berry tart?"

"Delish!" Charity took a teensy-weensy bite of her piece. "I just love Bluedazzle berries." Rarity looked down at the tart on

Charity's plate. She had barely eaten a single berry. That was odd.

Charity pushed her plate away. "So what do you want to know about me?"

"*Everything.*" Rarity leaned forward. "Your favorite new trends, the best piece you've ever made, what products you use on your beautiful mint mane—you know, *the usual* important topics." Rarity looked down at the H.O.O.F. program's brochure. Rarity wasn't quite Rainbow Dash in the competitiveness department, but she did love a good challenge now and then. "But first, you can start by telling me about this fabulous H.O.O.F. fashion competition."

"The competition?" Charity clammed up. She took a timid sip of her tea. "The competition is where all the apprentices present their own line—the one they worked on with their mentors. The winner gets to display their designs in the fall windows at Sack's and possibly even gets to be in *Mare Eclair.*"

"Are you serious?!" Rarity stood up and put her hooves out on the table. Her eyes looked huge. "WE. MUST. WIN."

Sack's was one of the biggest, most luxurious department stores in Manehattan. It got tons of hoof traffic from all the city ponies and tourists who visited just to see the elaborate window displays. It would be unbelievable exposure for a budding designer like Charity. Or even a seasoned one like Rarity at that. Why, if *she'd* had the chance to display her designs there, she would be over the moon! And a magazine spread? Well, that would just be icing on the cupcake.

"I'm getting the vibe that you're not as thrilled about this idea as I am. Can I ask why, dear? It's *Sacks,* for Celestia's sake!"

"Because there's totally no way I'll *ever* win!" Charity explained. She turned her gaze out the window. "The other ponies in my program are so talented. I mean, I know that I'll learn so much from you. But I don't think I'll ever measure up to them, even *with* your help."

"That attitude will simply not do!" Rarity said as her face morphed into a frown. She stood up and began to use her magic to move the tea set to the sink and fill the sink with bubbles and suds. After a moment, she turned around theatrically and proclaimed, "Stick with me, Charity, and you'll be in the spotlight in no time."

"You really think so?" Charity asked, biting her lip. "You think I have a shot to be an incredible, amazing, famous designer like you?"

The expression of admiration Charity wore was intoxicating. It was like Rarity's life was an outfit that lacked pizzazz and Charity was the long-sought-after accessory that completed it. She suddenly couldn't wait to share her secrets of success with the young pony.

"Of course, darling." Rarity smiled. "Just do exactly as I do."

CHAPTER 6

The Perfect Accessory

*** ***

"Why are you counting those ribbons?" Charity prodded. She was leaning in so close to Rarity that her mint-colored mane fell over Rarity's shoulder and onto the ribbon basket itself. Rarity scooted away. Maybe Charity was used to riding crowded hubway trains in Manehattan. But here in Ponyville, she clearly needed to learn a thing or two about personal space.

"I'm just checking inventory," Rarity said, standing up and backing farther away from Charity. "It's very crucial to make sure you have enough supplies when you're a designer in high demand." Rarity had to admit to herself that she was starting to sound very wise, even though she was making it all up as she went along. "One has to be ready at the drop of a fabulous hat."

"Drop of a fabulous hat," Charity repeated, scribbling something down on her scroll. In the lead-up to Charity's arrival, Rarity had been so busy thinking about what a great mentor she was going to be, she hadn't really made much of a plan for how exactly to do it. But so far, her strategy of looking as busy and important as possible was working.

For the past few days, Rarity fussed with things around the boutique, standing in attractive poses and making vague statements. Now and then, she would trot over to her stash of fabrics or her order ledger and go, "Hmmm, yes, yes…no!" and then pretend to scribble something down on a scroll. It was very convincing.

"Is there anything you need me to do?" Charity looked around anxiously. She trotted over to one of the choir dresses and started to take it off the dress form. "I could work on this for you. Maybe alter the hem and bring the sleeves up a bit? About two inches should do it, I think." Charity held the dress up to inspect it closer.

"NO!" Rarity shouted. "Get your hooves off!"

Charity dropped the gown in shock. "Sorry, I…"

"No, *I'm* sorry, darling." Rarity laughed nervously. She trotted over to pick up the garment, blushing. She was a little embarrassed at her outburst. "I'm just very protective of my work. You understand, right?"

"Of course," Charity nodded. "I never let any of my classmates touch my work. It's totally just another way that you and I are the same!"

"Right. The same," Rarity replied. She rearranged the dress and looked around for something acceptable for Charity to do with herself. A pile of fabric scraps lying in the corner was practically begging to be cleaned and organized. But, no, that wasn't very much fun. A bin filled with completed order scrolls needed alphabetizing and filing, but that seemed dull, too. Suddenly, the H.O.O.F. brochure on the table caught Rarity's eye again.

"Maybe we should try to start working on your fashion line for the competition!" Rarity exclaimed with delight. She loved starting new projects. It was finishing them that was actually the hard part. "It's perfect."

"Now?" Charity replied. Her eyes darted around. "But I—"

"Ah, ahh, ahhh," Rarity singsonged. "No time like the present to make today a beautiful gift." A little nagging voice in the back of Rarity's mind (that sounded a lot like Sweetie Belle) told her she should follow her own advice and put her muzzle to the grindstone with the choir dresses. But she was *supposed* to help Charity, she told herself. It was Rarity's duty as a H.O.O.F. mentor.

She recalled reading something about "the responsibility of being a part of the highest order of fashion excellence" to rationalize her actions, and sat Charity down with some scrolls and quills. Rarity cleared her throat. "Now, the best thing to do when starting a new line is to come up with an absolutely *extraordinary* topic."

"Come up with an extraordinary topic?" Charity repeated. She bit her lip and held her quill at the ready. "How do you do that?"

"I suppose I look at my surroundings and see what inspires me," Rarity said. The two ponies looked around the room. It was just a messy workshop. The only things in sight were fabric scraps, sewing tools, and a heap of unfinished choir dresses. Charity gave it a shot. "How about a line inspired by...spools of thread!"

Rarity giggled as an image of Pinkie Pie wearing a costume of a giant spool of thread danced through her head. It wasn't too far off from reality, seeing as Pinkie Pie was the only pony Rarity knew who owned a giant costume of herself.

"Let's give it another try, shall we?" Rarity said, looking around.

Charity was determined to get it right. She saw some clothes, a pot of tea, and a fluffy white kitty cat. "Oooh! How about outfits inspired by cats?" Charity suggested. "Or outfits *for* cats!"

Rarity winced. "Not *quite* what I had in mind, but it's okay. We're just getting started. It will all come together in the end,

I promise. Remember—when the going gets tough, the tough get sewing!"

"That's cute! I like that." Charity relaxed a bit and smiled. "What about teacups?" Charity said, looking down at her cup. Her face started to blush red. "Like sort of a fine china pattern look?"

"That's getting better, but it still needs more *pizzazz*," replied Rarity, reconsidering her teaching strategy.

Luckily, a bell ringing and a soft voice calling out from the front of the shop stopped her short. "Hello? Is anypony here?"

"Duty calls!" Rarity said, quickly standing up and trotting out of the room. "I think we have a customer!" Teaching was much more difficult than Rarity had anticipated. Any sort of distraction was a welcome one.

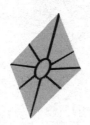

CHAPTER 7

Just Like Twins

$$\bigstar \quad \bigstar \quad \bigstar$$

The customer was Fluttershy. Except she wasn't there to buy anything and she wasn't really a customer. But those were just teensy-weensy details. Fluttershy had stopped by the boutique to invite Rarity and Charity to an afternoon picnic by the Ponyville Lake. Twilight Sparkle, Applejack, Rainbow Dash, and Pinkie Pie were all going to be there, along with their pets.

"If you're not too busy working on your project," Fluttershy said softly, "I think it could be really nice for Charity to come meet all our animal friends." She smiled at Charity, who seemed to be standing very close behind Rarity.

"How fun!" Charity exclaimed. "What do you think, Rarity?"

"Of course we'll attend," Rarity replied. It sounded *trés* relaxing! "We'll be sure to bring Opal." At the mention of her name, the fluffy white kitty purred and wove her way through Rarity's hooves. Charity bent down to pet the cat, but Opal hissed at her.

Rarity frowned. "Now, Opal, that's no way to treat a guest." The kitty pouted and ran over to Fluttershy, who had a gift when it came to animals.

"Poor little kitty-witty is stressed out, isn't she?" Fluttershy cooed. She leaned down and pet the kitty with her hoof. Opal began to purr again. "An afternoon outside will do you good, you sweet thing. I'll see you later!"

Once Fluttershy left, Rarity turned to her student with a look of glee on her face. "I do so love a garden party, don't you?"

"What am I going to wear?!" Charity squealed. She glanced at herself in the standing mirror that Rarity kept by the front door.

"I was wondering the exact same thing." Rarity nodded in agreement. It was so nice to have another fashion-minded pony around the place. "Now, what have you brought from Manehattan?" She batted her long eyelashes. It didn't hurt to ask. "Care to maybe…share?"

"Like, of course!" answered Charity before cantering off toward her luggage. "Anything for you, Rarity!"

"Well, what are we waiting for?" Rarity urged. "Bring on the clothes!"

It wasn't long until expensive clothes from the big city surrounded the two ponies. The Unicorns used their magic to make the garments dance around the room, creating different outfits. Rarity was in absolute style heaven.

"What do you think?" Charity said. She had brought items for every occasion imaginable. There were sweet sundresses and breezy jackets. There were gorgeous gowns and sequined scarves. There were items that came off the rack, along with one-of-a-kind haute couture pieces. A one-shouldered light green gown made of willowy organza was a particular standout. Rarity had never seen anything like it.

"I think everything is marvelous, but *who* designed this impeccable specimen of wearable art?" Rarity inspected the expert beadwork on the seams. It was so exquisite...so different from her own designs. She wished she had created it.

Charity quickly snatched it away. "Oh, that's nothing. Just something I...found." She tossed the dress into a suitcase and quickly snapped it shut.

"But where did—?"

"What about this?" Charity interrupted, holding up a wide-brimmed glittery sun hat finished with a purple, dip-dyed satin ribbon. "I just bought it in Neighcy's and it's…"

"…another Rarity original!" Rarity couldn't believe that the young pony had purchased so many of her wares from Manehattan department stores. Charity smiled and put on the hat.

"I found your matching one over in the closet. I hope you don't mind." Charity put the second hat on Rarity's head and giggled. "We'll be just like twins!"

Rarity looked at the two of them side by side in the mirror. If it weren't for her green mane, Charity *would* almost be her twin. It made Rarity feel strange, but she wasn't sure why.

"What do you think?" Charity looked hopeful. "Can I pull it off?"

Rarity smiled. "Absolutely, darling."

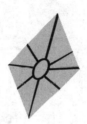

CHAPTER 8

A Big Splash

★ ★ ★

By the time they got to the lake, the picnic was already in full swing. Applejack and Rainbow Dash were taking turns doing cannonballs into the water. Rainbow's tortoise, Tank, and Applejack's scruffy brown farm dog, Winona, happily watched from the side.

"Are you ready for the biggest splash Ponyville's ever seen?!" Rainbow Dash hollered before careening into the lake. Winona barked. Tank blinked . . . very slowly.

Droplets of water landed on Fluttershy, who was feeding Angel Bunny some fresh carrots. "Oh, that's okay," she said, even though Rainbow hadn't apologized. Angel Bunny crossed his tiny arms, annoyed. He was very protective of his pony. "Be a good bunny and sit down, Angel. I brought you a cherry!"

Over on the grass, Twilight Sparkle was reading aloud from a book. " 'Household Spells, Chapter Six—Clean It and Mean It!' " Spike and Owlowiscious were both trying to listen but seemed to be nodding off to sleep.

"We've arrived!" Rarity announced with a grand flourish. Charity was at her side.

Rarity struck a pose, and Charity was quick to mimic it.

"I'm so glad you two could make it." Twilight smiled. "I was worried that you'd have too much work to do back at the boutique." She trotted up to greet them, and Spike roused himself to follow close behind.

"Hi, Charity!" the dragon yelled enthusiastically. Rarity shot him a look. "Oh, and, uh, Rarity, you're looking really nice today," he quickly added. "Good to see you!"

"Thank you, Spike," Rarity replied, looking a bit sore. "We are very busy and important, but sunshine and time with friends always do wonders for creativity, no?" Rarity put on her teal cat's-eye sunglasses. Charity produced a similar pair from her saddlebag and put them on, too. "So I thought, *Why not?*"

"Um…*indeed,*" Charity echoed, nodding. "Why not?"

Twilight raised an eyebrow at the posh accent Charity seemed to be putting on along with her sunglasses. It was a little eerie. With their matching curled manes, the soft white of their marshmallow coats, and their light blue cutie marks being so similar—the two ponies almost looked like clones. If it weren't for their manes, Twilight would have thought that Rarity had fallen into the Mirror Pool and duplicated herself just like Pinkie Pie had once done.

"Thanks for popping by, girls!" Pinkie Pie bounded over. She had brought along her new popcorn popper and was whipping up a fresh batch of "Pinkie's Popped Candy Pinkcorn." It was a tasty mixture of pink popcorn topped with gumdrops, sprinkles, and chocolate chips. "Have some Pinkcorn! It's scrumptiously yummy for your tummy!" She tossed them each a box, and they began to munch on it.

"Simply delectable!" said Rarity, through mouthfuls of the treat.

"Yes, simply delectable!" parroted Charity. She was still trying hard to put on a posh accent like her mentor. Applejack trotted up to join them, still dripping wet from her last cannonball. "Good to have ya, Charity!" She tipped her cowgirl hat, which was also wet. "Care to join in our little contest, girls?"

"Oooh!" Charity was actually really great at cannonballs. It was a secret talent from her fillyhood. She took off her hat and started to get ready.

"You can count *me* out." Rarity wrinkled her nose and turned her head away. "I simply could not mess up this amazing look I'm sporting with some murky lake water. But of course, you can join if you'd like...." She looked at the young pony expectantly.

Charity's eyes darted from the water back to Applejack, and then to the look on Rarity's face. "You're right." She put her hat back on. "Better not. Lake water is disgusting."

"Are you sure, Charity?" Twilight Sparkle said in concern. "It seems like you wanted to try it."

"Nope, I'm good!" Charity replied before quickly correcting herself. "I mean—no, thank you, *darling*."

"If you insist," replied Twilight, trying to make sense of Rarity and Charity's student/teacher dynamic. It was clear that Charity was learning *something* from her mentor. Just maybe not the right things.

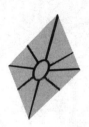

CHAPTER 9

DeSigner's Block

✷ ✷ ✷

Rarity was busy reclining in a deck chair. She closed her eyes and felt the glorious sunshine on her face. She was just starting to doze off into a glorious dream about designing the costumes for Sapphire Shores's new tour when Twilight Sparkle interrupted her. "So, how are things going with Charity?"

"She enjoys the finer things in life, so naturally things are going great," Rarity replied. She was slightly perturbed at being disturbed. "Did you know her favorite designer is also Coco Cheval? And we have the same favorite model—Honey Flanks. We have so much in common!"

"Yeah, it certainly *seems* that way." Twilight laughed. She looked over at Charity, who was lying in the exact same position as Rarity on an identical chair.

"What is it?" Rarity sat up. "I know you have something to say. Out with it!"

"I just worry that maybe Charity is taking her admiration for you a little too far." Twilight shrugged. Rainbow Dash jumped into the water, and Charity squealed in horror as a droplet fell onto her mane. "Look at her: She's being...*you*."

"I have no idea what you're talking about," Rarity said defensively. Even though the very same thought had recently crossed her mind, Rarity was never going to come right out and admit it to Twilight Sparkle. It would be like Rarity was declaring her own failure as a teacher!

Charity, like Rarity's other projects, was just a work in progress. Rarity lowered her sunglasses. "She just looks like a classy, sophisticated pony. There is nothing wrong with that, Twilight." She turned her nose up in the air as if it punctuated her point.

"Just be careful," Twilight urged, eyeing Charity as she flipped open *Mare Éclair*. The pony on the cover was a model named Glitzi Grooms, and it promised tips on deep mane conditioners, cutie mark tints, and the hottest new hoof charms from Saddle Arabia.

"Quick! Somepony hide me!" Rarity shrieked, and dived into a nearby bush.

"What's goin' on, Rarity?" Applejack shouted from the water. "Did ya see a rattlesnake?"

"Rarity!" Charity cried out. She ran over to the bush. "Are you all right?!"

"Shhh!" Rarity hissed. "I don't want her to hear!" After a few moments had passed, Rarity peeped her head out from in between the leaves. "Is she gone? Can I come out?"

"Is who gone? Why are you acting so weird, Rarity?" Rainbow Dash laughed. "I mean, weirder than usual." Applejack shrugged. A pony could never really predict what would send Rarity into a tizzy.

"It was Golden Harvest! I saw her walking across the grass and I can't..." Rarity stage-whispered, craning her neck in all directions to make sure the coast was clear. When she was sure the pony in question was out of earshot, she emerged. "I simply *cannot* see her!"

Rainbow Dash and Applejack exchanged a look. Whatever her reason for avoiding the pony, it must have been important. Rarity wouldn't risk getting her coat dirty for just anything. "Come on, sugarcube," Applejack urged. "Spit it out!"

Rarity's lip quivered. "It's terribly tragic! I am supposed to deliver the Ponyville Choir dresses to her by next week and I...I..."

"You..." Pinkie Pie took a deep breath. "...are totally behind on them because you hate what you designed and you're stuck and you thought having an apprentice would help but you're also not really sure how to teach her and now you're embarrassed 'cause you have no dresses and no clue what you're doing?"

Charity's jaw dropped. None of the other ponies looked surprised at Pinkie's revelation. She was scarily accurate with her guesses.

"Oh, Pinkie! It's truuuuee!" Rarity cried. "Charity, darling! Don't look at me! I didn't want you to see me like this. I have..." She looked down at the ground and then back up at them. "...DESIGNER'S BLOCK!"

Charity gasped. Pinkie Pie gasped. It was always better when more than one pony gasped in a dramatic situation.

"Not designer's block!" Charity shook her head in despair.

"Toodles, my dear. You might as well pack your bags and head home." Rarity sniffed. "I'm sure you don't want to idolize—I mean, *learn* from me anymore... now that you know what I truly am. A *failure!*" Rarity collapsed onto Twilight's picnic blanket. She let out a hearty sob.

Charity blinked a few times, her expression blank. Then a wide grin began to spread across her face. "Forget my H.O.O.F. project! Let's finish those dresses!"

"Really?" Rarity said, perking up. "You want to stay?"

"Of course!" Charity nodded. She turned to the other ponies. "It's like this saying I came up with: '*When the going gets tough, the tough get sewing!*'"

Everypony laughed. Rarity frowned. That was not Charity's saying—it was *Rarity*'s! How dare she?

"Good one, Charity!" Pinkie Pie giggled.

"You sure are clever, sugarcube," said Applejack. "This is some apprentice you've got here!"

"Yes, she certainly is...." Rarity said, narrowing her eyes. She had thought Twilight Sparkle had gotten Charity all wrong, but now she wasn't so sure. What sort of pony would just steal the fabulous words out of another pony's mouth without giving them credit?

Rarity was annoyed. But as her saying went, it was time to get sewing. Plus, she wasn't really in a position to refuse the extra help right now. Rarity sighed and took off her sun hat. "We have work to do!"

she announced, and trotted off toward the Carousel Boutique.

"We have work to do!" Charity smiled wide at the other ponies. She took off her hat with the same flourish that she'd just seen her mentor do.

"Rarity, wait up!"

CHAPTER 10

Dyeing to Please

★ ★ ★

Over the next few days, the two designers got down to business. Charity always seemed to know what Rarity was thinking, even before she said it. If she needed a rotary cutter, it appeared instantly at her worktable. When her hem tape ran low, Charity replenished it. And if Rarity was thirsty, a cup of fresh tea somehow made its way into her hoof. It was like a new kind of magic, without using any magic at all. Their minds were on the same wavelength. Which was especially annoying because Rarity wanted to stay mad at Charity, but she just couldn't.

"What have I been doing all this time without an assistant?" Rarity wondered aloud. "Twilight has always had Spike around and no wonder! It's like a dream." She lifted a finished dress back onto its ponnequin dress form. "Here's another one down!"

"Another one down!" echoed Charity, smiling. She trotted over and fluffed the skirt of the dress so that it lay perfectly. She made a check mark on her scroll. "Do you need anything else?" Charity asked eagerly, trotting over to Rarity and leaning in about an inch away from her face. "How about some more tea? Another bobbin? A back massage? A tail braid?" Twilight's warning suddenly sprang to mind. Maybe the two of them did need to spend a little time apart.

"My goodness," Rarity said, suddenly feeling a little cramped. "Is it hot in here?"

"Should I open a window?" Charity asked. "Or I could totally sit here and fan you." Charity somehow procured a giant leaf and started fanning her.

"Where did you get that?" Rarity asked, raising an eyebrow.

"Pinkie Pie." Charity smiled. "Who got it from the Ponyville fan shop. She gave it to me when she stopped by to lend me her pinking shears the other day."

"Oh, that makes sense." Rarity nodded, inspecting her apprentice. Charity looked tired. She had a slightly crazy look in her eye, and her mint-colored mane was becoming a little wild. It was like she would stop at nothing to please Rarity. Maybe Rarity had been a little bit harsh about the whole "stealing her words" thing. It was kind of a silly thing to get one's mane in a twist over.

"Charity, you've done more than enough for now." She adjusted her red work glasses. "You should go out and do something fun! Just run a few errands on this list, and then the afternoon is yours." Rarity handed her a little scroll with some items written on it.

"Are you sure?" Charity asked. "I could always stay here and reorganize your fabrics again. The organzas and brocades are looking a little untidy...."

"No, no, no! I will not hear another word about it—shoo!" Rarity pushed the pony out the door. Once she was gone, Rarity breathed a little, tiny sigh of relief. It was hard work being somepony's role model.

Charity was having a busy afternoon. She'd stopped by Sweet Apple Acres for some apples, Sugarcube Corner for some Bluedazzle berry tarts, Fluttershy's cottage for some kitty food, and the Golden Oak Library for some old book on traditional period costume design. The last stop had eaten up a lot of time because Twilight Sparkle tried to get Charity to take some extra books about Star Swirl the Bearded and an art book about seaponies for "fashion inspiration."

She'd finally just taken them to be polite. That Twilight Sparkle could be very persistent. For that matter, so could Spike, who'd offered to accompany Charity on the rest of her errands at least four times. She'd politely declined.

Now Charity was wandering around town, looking for somewhere to buy the last thing on her list—quills. When she found the sign for the Quills and Sofas shop, she trotted over. It seemed so odd. She peeked inside the window to see if they really sold only those two things. Sure enough, the shelves on the walls were lined with quills and the floor was packed with sofas of every shape and color.

"Interesting," she marveled aloud to nopony. "The suburbs are such a mystery!" She was about to go inside, but as she leaned back from the window, she noticed her mane in the reflection. It looked awfully frizzy and unkempt. *How dreadful,* she thought. If she wanted to be more like Rarity, a messy mane was not the way to do it. Rarity would say, "An untidy mane equals a plain Jane." Something had to be done, and fast.

"Excuse me, sir," Charity said to a tall red stallion with a green apple cutie mark she saw passing by. "You wouldn't happen to know where a mare can find a beauty salon around here, would you?"

"Eeyup," replied Big Mac. He was hitched up to his applecart. He appeared to be in the middle of making a delivery to Mayor Mare at the Ponyville town hall. She could tell because the crates read MAYOR MARE, TOWN HALL.

"Oh awesome!" replied Charity. "I mean… how *divine*." She batted her eyelashes like she'd seen Rarity do. "My mane is totally appalling, don't you think?"

Big Mac wasn't a stallion of many sayings. "Nope." He shook his head.

Charity blushed, taking it as a compliment. "Thanks. So anyway, where is it?" He pointed his hoof down the lane to a building with a purple roof and tall gold-tipped spires. The green sign hanging out front had a picture of a mare with a beautiful, flowing gold mane and tail.

"Thank you *ever* so much!" She smiled gratefully and took off. *"Au revoir!"*

"Eeyup," he said, and continued on his way.

Once inside, a pink pony with a slicked-back blue mane and a white headband greeted her. "Welcome to the Ponyville Day Spa," said the pony.

A blue pony with a pink mane walked up to join them. "I'm Lotus Blossom," she said. "What can we do for you today? We have mud masks, hooficures, wing massages, Canterlot mane relaxers, and even more!" Lotus Blossom did a grand sweeping gesture with her hoof to show off the gorgeous space. It was like heaven.

"That all sounds amazing." Charity brightened. She wanted everything on the list but probably only had time for one beauty treatment. She had to make it count. "Definitely something for my mane."

"How about a cut?" the first pony suggested, running her hooves through Charity's beautiful mint locks.

"Or a perm?" Lotus Blossom offered, circling around her.

"I have an even better idea!" Charity smiled. Rarity was going to be so impressed when she saw. "Tell me, do you ponies do mane coloring here?"

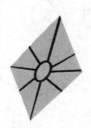

CHAPTER 11

The Sweet Sounds of Success

★ ★ ★

"Voilà!" Rarity announced as she lifted up the final dress with her magic. It had turned out that peace and quiet was just what Rarity needed to finish. Charity was a great help to the boutique, but her attention could also be a little suffocating. It was a little bit like having Sweetie Belle around.

But Rarity couldn't help it if younger ponies looked up to her. It just came with the territory of being adored.

"Opal, aren't they spectacular?" She made the dress rotate slowly, like it was sitting on a motorized display in a store-front, surrounded by the magic light. The sequined ribbon sparkled. Opalescence, who was napping, opened one eye and meowed her approval. Just like her pony, the kitty was the picture of sophistication. She even wore a tiny starched purple bow atop her head.

"So glad you agree, Opal. Not too showy, yet still utterly fabulous. Thank goodness I'm finished." Rarity looked at the clock on the wall. "And with time to spare! The concert doesn't start for hours. I have

plenty of time to treat myself to a hooficure at the Day Spa before the dresses
need to be delivered. I deserve it." She took
off her red work glasses and got out a little scroll to scribble a note for her absent
apprentice.

Dearest Charity,
Beauty emergency!!
Will be back soon to bring
the dresses to the concert.
Hope you had fun
around town!
XOxoxoxoxoxo, Rarity

Charity arrived at the Sweet Sounds of Summer concert with just an hour left until showtime. She was now completely out of breath, and her mane didn't look quite as perfect as when she'd left the spa. Twenty choir dresses and fifteen bow ties were much heavier than she had guessed, even with the aid of Unicorn magic. But it was worth it. Rarity was going to be so proud that she'd taken it upon herself to bring them to the show for her. Plus, her newly dyed purple mane and tail looked amazing. Just like her idol: Rarity. She couldn't wait to show her!

"I'm here! I'm here!" Charity shouted as she ran behind the curtain that had been set up as a backstage area. "I've got the dresses and bow ties."

"Thank Celestia!" said Golden Harvest, an Earth pony whose cutie mark of a bunch of carrots matched her orange mane and tail. She turned to the rest of the group and shouted at the other choir members. "Rarity's here, everypony! Time for a costume change!"

"Oh, I'm not Rar—" Charity said, but she was quickly interrupted by a flood of excited comments from the ensemble.

"Wow, Rarity! You've really outdone yourself this time." Lyra Heartstrings took her dress and hugged it close to her body. "I want to wear it every day!"

"Such attention to detail!" added Twinkleshine, a pink-maned Unicorn. She held up the hem of the frock to admire the expert hoofiwork.

"Such pretty ribbon!" said a Pegasus. The sight of the green dress against her purple coat reminded Charity of Twilight's dragon friend Spike.

"Such beautiful sparkles," said Tippy Tappy. She put her ukulele down to examine the garment. "It's a real showstopper!"

"I have to say, Miss Rarity"—Senior Mint, a tall green Pegasus, trotted over to Charity and held up his green bow tie—"I do like the color." He winked, because it was the very same hue as his coat.

Charity knew it wasn't right to let them believe she was totally responsible for the dresses, but it felt so wonderful to hear them singing her praises! All she'd ever wanted was to be like Rarity. And now here she was with ponies thinking that she *was* Rarity. It was too amazing to give up just yet.

"Oh, thank you so much, everypony," Charity beamed. She tried to imagine what Rarity would say if she were here. "I just felt so... *inspired* by your gorgeous voices!"

"Well, they look stunning. They were worth the wait!" said Golden Harvest, reappearing in the gown. The emerald color looked very pretty against her orange mane. She started to head toward the stage when she turned around and gave Charity a double take. "Say, Rarity, something's different about you. I can't quite put my hoof on it."

Charity gave a nervous laugh. This had been a terrible idea, but there was no turning back now. She put on her best Rarity voice and replied, "Whatever do you mean, darling?" Charity fluffed her newly dyed purple mane, batted her eyelashes, and hoped for the best.

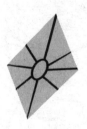

CHAPTER 12

The ugly Truth

✳ ✳ ✳

"My costumes for the concert have been stolen!" Rarity howled. She paced around the boutique anxiously. There were only forty-five minutes until she was supposed to deliver them to the Ponyville Choir members, and they had just vanished. "All that hard work down the drain. And my reputation—*ruined*!"

"Stolen?" asked Rainbow Dash. "Are you sure?"

"Yes, I'm sure!" Rarity replied. "Vanished!"

"Maybe Sweetie Belle decided to tidy up again and just moved them?" suggested Fluttershy, even though she knew that scenario was unlikely. Sweetie Belle would surely never make the mistake of moving Rarity's work things again after the response she got last time.

"No, they were pilfered, pinched…purloined!" Rarity yelped. She threw her hooves up in the air. "However you want to say it! All I know is it spells *DOOMED*. D-O-O-M-E-D."

"Want me to do a quick scan of Ponyville

from the sky?" said Rainbow Dash. "I can catch the thief!" Rainbow seemed excited at the prospect. She put her hooves up in a boxing position. "I'll take 'em down!"

"No…" Rarity whimpered. Where was Charity when she needed a tissue? That girl had been gone a long time. "I must face this like a true professional." Rarity's face became grave. "I am going to go to the concert and tell Golden Harvest the truth. Even it is…ugly!"

"Ten minutes to showtime, everypony!" Rarity heard Golden Harvest call out to her choir members behind the curtain. Rarity had finally made her way to the backstage area after nudging through a massive crowd of townsponies who had come out to watch the show. Her heart was beating like crazy. She didn't want to tell the ponies that there would be no beautiful dresses and no bold bow ties. They had counted on her. The only thing worse than a tragic outfit was letting ponies down.

Rarity smoothed down her mane, took a deep breath, and pushed back the red velvet curtain. *This is it—the end of my career,* she thought.

"I regret to inform you all that there will be no dresses! They have been stolen," she announced with a grave tone. She kept her eyes closed. "Please accept my deepest apologies." She expected the sounds of crying, but her words were met with giggles. When she looked up, half the choir was standing in front of her, wearing their costumes. The very ones she had sewn. But how? Rarity rubbed her eyes in disbelief.

"Rarity, you're a hoot!" said Twinkleshine. She smoothed down the skirt on her green dress and trotted off to join a group that was singing warm-up scales. Senior Mint blew into a pitch pipe and they all began to sing. *"Fill-ee-ee-ee! Fill-ee-ee-ee! Fill-ee-ee-ee!"*

"But how did you? But I thought that they...!" Rarity stammered. "Where did you get these?" It was a fashion miracle!

"You brought them, of course." Golden Harvest made a face.

"I did?" Rarity felt a bit faint. Was she losing her mind?

Tippy Tappy put a hoof on her shoulder. "Rarity, are you okay? You look a little green."

"I'm perfectly fine now," Rarity lied. "I guess I should let you get on with the show....Break a leg!" She laughed nervously as she backed toward the curtain and exited. On her way out, she heard somepony call her name again. She popped her head back in again.

"Yes?" Rarity said, peeking through the folds of velvet.

"Yes?" said another pony nearby at the same time. It was a white pony with a dark purple mane and tail, just like her. "Did somepony need something from *moi*— Rarity?"

"I just wanted to know if you could redo my bow tie," a brown stallion named Coconut said. He leaned down as the pony helped him. When she was finished, he said, "Thanks, Rarity! Never could figure those things out."

The pony giggled. "Anytime, darling!"

Rarity's eyes grew wide in shock. Somepony was impersonating her! The pony's back was to her, so she couldn't see the culprit's face. She craned her neck to get a better view and accidentally leaned so far forward that she tumbled straight through the curtain!

"Rarity!" Charity said, running over to her. "Are you all right?"

All Rarity could see was purple. Same gorgeous purple mane. Same fabulous purple tail. Was she looking into a mirror? No, definitely not. She was looking at the imposter—and it was none other than Charity herself!

"Just WHAT do you think you're doing, missy?!" Rarity screeched as she stood up and brushed herself off. "Is this some sort of joke? Take off those wigs this instant!"

"They aren't wigs." Charity looked down at the dirt. "I dyed my mane and tail at the Ponyville Day Spa. I thought you would think it looked fabulous."

"Well, I do, yes. It does," Rarity admitted, momentarily forgetting the argument and only thinking of how nice her hairstyle looked, even on another pony. "But only on *me*! And that doesn't explain why you stole the costumes."

"Five minutes until showtime!" Golden Harvest announced to the backstage area, reminding Rarity that they were in public.

Luckily, nopony had noticed the duo yet.

They were all too busy getting ready to go onstage. Rarity glanced around, suddenly paranoid that she and Charity were going to become a spectacle. They did look almost identical with their white coats and matching hair—the only differences were the colors of their eyes and the shapes of their cutie marks. Rarity's was three diamonds and Charity's was three heart-shaped gems. Still, they were both light blue.

"I was only trying to help, I swear!" Charity explained. "I brought them over because you were running late. And I *so* understand the importance of a beauty emergency, so I was not about to interrupt that." She looked up at Rarity like a puppy who'd been caught playing in the mud just after a bubble bath.

"I was just filling in until you got here,"

Charity whimpered. "We—you worked so hard and I wanted to make sure your beautiful work arrived in time."

"Thank you, dear." Rarity softened a bit. "Just don't take anything else without telling me again. Okay?"

"Okay." Charity nodded as a pretty melody began to play. "The show is starting!"

"Shall we?" Rarity said, motioning to the velvet curtain. "Just stay in the back. I don't want anypony to see us like this. Celestia knows what that would do for my reputation."

Rarity and Charity crept out into the back of the crowd. The choir ponies looked magnificent in their costumes. The Ponyville Choir started singing their first song entitled "Breezy in the Wind." Golden Harvest stepped forward to sing a solo: *"And it seems to trees, you've spread your wings, like a Breezy in the wind...*" She did a twirl, and the beautiful dress billowed out, the glittered green ribbon details catching the light. Everypony ooohed and aahed.

"My dresses are amazing!" Charity said, completely mesmerized. "I mean, *our* dresses," she quickly corrected. Rarity raised an eyebrow at her apprentice. She began to wonder what sort of show Charity herself was putting on.

CHAPTER 13

The Similarity of Charity

✶✶✶

"Thank you all for joining me here today," Rarity said gravely. Applejack, Pinkie Pie, Rainbow Dash, Fluttershy, and Twilight Sparkle were all gathered around her in the main hall of the Castle of the Two Sisters. It was the only place that Rarity could think of where Charity wouldn't find them. "I'm afraid there is a crisis."

"What's the matter?" Twilight Sparkle said. "Whatever it is, we're here for you. True friends stick together."

"Thank you, Twilight. That means so much." Rarity looked across at her best friends appreciatively. They were always there to help in a crisis, especially Spike. Who wasn't here. "Hey, where is Spike?"

"He said he had a prior engagement." Twilight shrugged. "Whoever knows what that little dragon is up to?"

"Go on, sugarcube." Applejack turned back to Rarity. "What is it?"

"Is Opal sick again?" Fluttershy asked, eyes wide with worry. "She did seem a little sniffly at the picnic. This is all my fault!"

"Psht!" Rainbow Dash scoffed. "Ten bits

says it has something to do with that wannabe Charity."

"I bet you *eleven* bits!" Pinkie Pie shouted like an old-timey auctioneer having a great time. "Eleven bits, ten bits! Twelve bits! Eleven bits! Going, going, gone...to Rainbow Dash for eleven bits!"

"That's not really how that works...." Rainbow Dash shook her head.

"Is that true?" Twilight Sparkle stepped forward, ignoring Pinkie. "Is something wrong with Charity?"

"Yes!" Rarity cried out. "I think she's trying to *STEAL. MY. LIFE!*" She collapsed onto the floor in a heap but quickly jumped back up. "Ugh! That doesn't work as well without a sofa nearby."

"Well, I wasn't gonna say anythin', but since you bring it up," Applejack said, "the other day, Charity came by Sweet Apple Acres for some apples. She wanted me to teach her how to buck a tree."

"Scandalous!" Pinkie Pie said. "She's stealing Applejack's life, too."

"No, just the opposite!" Applejack shook her head. "She was having a great time bucking apples, but the youngin' refused to do it anymore once she found out that Rarity ain't a fan. Said somethin' about gettin' too dirty and ran for the hills."

Rarity gasped. "See?"

"And she wouldn't join in our cannonball contest!" Rainbow Dash added. "Even though she totally wanted to."

"You know…" Pinkie Pie put on her detective hat and took out her bubble pipe. She was in full detective mode, pacing back and forth. "Charity actually came by the bakery the other day and requested Bluedazzle berry tarts! Mmmmhmmm, yep, I knew it."

"What does that tell us, Pinkie?" Twilight asked. "She likes sweets? So do I...."

"Bluedazzle berry tarts are my favorite; she doesn't even like them!" Rarity exclaimed. "I know because I made a tart, and she barely ate any—oh wait, I told her to pick some of those up." Rarity laughed guiltily. "Whoopsies."

"I see...." Pinkie Pie raised an eyebrow and scribbled something down on a notepad.

"You've been awfully quiet," Rarity said, pointing to Fluttershy. Everypony looked at her expectantly. "Have you noticed anything...suspicious about my apprentice?" She trotted over and tried to do the "Fluttershy stare" to extract information out of her.

"Well…" Fluttershy said softly. She shrank back, retreating under her light pink mane like a turtle going into its shell. "Charity did stop by and ask me if I had any little white kittens she could adopt. She wanted one who looked just like Opal."

"See, Rarity?" Twilight sighed. "This is what I was trying to tell you at the picnic. Charity has it all backward! She thinks that if she copies you, she'll become the type of pony she looks up to."

"This is the worst possible thing!" Rarity moaned. First, Charity had stolen her saying, then she'd dyed her mane and tail to look exactly like her, and now she was adopting an identical cat? How would Charity like it if somepony copied her? Suddenly, Rarity had an idea. She took off for the castle exit. "Bye, girls!"

"Wait! Where are you going?" Rainbow Dash shouted after her.

Rarity stopped and looked over her shoulder. "How can I be a 'Rarity' if there's two of me? By very definition, that means I have to be unique! I've been so blind. I must set things straight again. I'm just going to have to show Charity how great it is to be herself." Then she cantered out the door.

"Hey, Rainbow," Pinkie Pie said. "I think you owe me eleven bits!"

Chapter 14

Purple and Green

★ ★ ★

After looking all over Ponyville, Rarity finally found the Unicorn and the dragon out searching for gems. She watched from afar as Charity bent down to pat Spike on the head. "My adorable little Spikey-Wikey! You're such a big help with these gems."

Rarity felt a sudden pang of jealousy.

That was *her* Spikey-Wikey! But then, she remembered her plan. She adjusted her mint-colored wig and smoothed down the light green dress she'd found in Charity's suitcase. She was ready.

"Anything for you, Charity!" Spike said, hearts still in his eyes. "I know my way around a gem cart. I've had a lot of practice with Rarity. She's the best at finding gems." The cart Spike was dragging only had a few shimmering stones inside—an emerald and a few aquamarines. Apparently, Charity didn't have as much of a knack for locating sapphires and rubies as Rarity did. There were some talents a pony couldn't fake.

"I know!" Charity nodded. "That's why I have to practice if I'm going to be as good as her someday. Tell me, what else does Rarity do?" They walked along casually and

Rarity followed, unnoticed. She was going to interrupt them, but she loved listening to conversations about herself, especially when they were complimentary.

"Let's see..." said Spike, scratching his claw on his scaly chin. "Well, for starters, she always looks pretty."

"Check!" Charity said, fluffing her purple mane. "What else?"

"And she always puts her friends first! Rarity is the most generous pony in all of Equestria." Spike reached for the emerald from the cart. "Can I have this?"

"Yes, you may!" Charity replied with a satisfied smile. "See? Generous! Did you know that 'Charity' means generosity? That's got to count for something, right?"

"Definitely!" Spike nodded, crunching into the emerald and swallowing it in one big gulp. "So can I have another one?" He grabbed one of the aquamarines and popped it into his mouth. "Oh, and she always tries to show her unique style. Rarity is her own pony."

It was the perfect cue. "Yes, she is!" Rarity called out, trotting over to them with a grand flourish. She did a spin to model the light green dress. The gauzy organza billowed and floated in the breeze. The beadwork on the seams caught the sunlight in just the right way.

"Wow, Rarity!" Spike said. "You look amazing!"

"That's my dress!" Charity cried, touching the fabric. "Why are you wearing that? I worked so hard on it!" Then she noticed Rarity's mint-colored mane and tail wigs. "And your mane! You dyed it?" Charity touched her own purple hair. "But I thought that purple was in?"

"I thought I'd try something new," Rarity posed. "What? You don't think it's fabulous?" She flipped the green mane over her shoulder.

"Well, I do, but it's just that...that you are..." Charity stammered. "It's like you're trying to look exactly like me!" Charity frowned and touched her mane. "Or how I *used* to look..." Charity slumped down. "Before I started trying to be you."

"Don't worry." Rarity smiled. She was glad that Charity was starting to see her point. "I can hardly blame you for coveting my style. But, Charity, darling," said Rarity as she took off the wigs and let her purple locks tumble out, "I would *never* dye my mane."

"Oh, Rarity, I'm so totally sorry!" Charity

exclaimed. She put her hoof to her head. "I've been, like, the worst apprentice in all of Equestria."

"I haven't been the best teacher, either," Rarity admitted. She put her hoof on Charity's shoulder. "I should have been helping you with your project instead of using you for my own personal career gain. I've set such a poor example. I did tell you to do as I did. I only realize now what a big mistake that was!" Rarity let out a massive sigh. "Frankly, I don't deserve to be a H.O.O.F. mentor."

"Are you kidding?" Charity smiled. "This whole experience has been so incredible. To watch you working in your element! It's totally everything I ever hoped for." She stepped close to Rarity. "You're the greatest fashion designer of all time, Rarity."

"That's so sweet." Rarity was so touched that she was starting to get a little choked up. "You're well on your way, too. This gown is simply stunning." She motioned to her outfit. "It's different from anything I have ever seen. If you keep at it, you're going to be a smashing success."

"Thank you!" Charity said, embracing Rarity in a hug. When they pulled apart, Charity said, "Can we start over?"

"Absolutely!" Rarity giggled. She stuck out her hoof. "It's nice to meet you; I'm Rarity."

"And I'm Charity Sweetmint. But you can call me 'Charity.'" Charity laughed, head held high. "Want to go to the spa with me? I think I might need to have my mane redone...."

"Only if we work on your fashion line

for the H.O.O.F. competition after!" Rarity said. "Just tell me what to do and I'll help. You're the boss!"

"Deal!" Charity nodded. "I even think I have an idea for it! It was inspired by something I saw in one of Twilight Sparkle's books."

"Sounds lovely!"

As the two ponies walked to the Ponyville Day Spa together, Charity had a smile plastered on her face. It was so much better to be herself than to try to be somepony else. Charity couldn't believe her mentor thought she had talent! She was already beginning to feel more comfortable in her own coat.

"Hey!" Charity turned to Spike and whispered, "Rarity thinks I have potential, Spikey-Wikey!"

"Ahem." Rarity cleared her throat. "Darling?"

Charity stopped. "Yes?"

"Let's get one thing straight. That's *my* Spikey-Wikey. *Capiche?*"

CHAPTER 15

A Sparkling Sensation

★ ★ ★

Charity adjusted the aqua-colored gown again and furrowed her brow. "Does it look better now, Rarity? It has to be, like, perfect." She brushed her minty mane away from her face and inspected her work.

"Up a little higher on the left," Rarity

said from across the tiny window space. "You *must* make sure the customers can see the adorable shells you added to the sweetheart neckline." Rarity was busy re-arranging another one of Charity's designs from her "Sparkling Sea" line, inspired by the mysterious and magical world of seaponies.

Charity adjusted the dress and stepped back to look at the whole collection. The fabrics were all deep ocean blues and pur-ples fading into swirly seaweed greens. The panels and pleats on the dresses looked almost like scaly fins—sparkly and fluid like the reflection of sunlight in water. It was a truly beautiful sight to behold.

"I still can't believe we're here at Sacks! With a fashion line that I designed!" Charity took a deep breath. The feeling was electric. It was almost too exciting to take. "Sorry, I meant that *we* designed." She giggled. She waved to Fluttershy and Pinkie Pie, who were outside the window modeling some of her shell jewelry. They had offered to help draw some of the hoof traffic in to look at the window display. Applejack, Rainbow, and Twilight were inside the store doing the same. "As a team."

"No, darling, this one was all you," Rarity said with a smile, walking up next to her protégé. "I was just there to guide you." Rarity cocked her head to the side with a sneaky grin on her face. "Personally, I think the extra boost of inspiration you got was from all those Bluedazzle berry tarts I made you eat while you worked."

Charity winced at the memory. "Rarity, I have a confession. . . ." she said hesitantly. "I absolutely detest Bluedazzle berries!"

"I know, darling," Rarity replied with a wink and a smile. "I know."

Howdy, partner!
Don't miss

my LITTLE PONY Applejack

Exclusive GIANT trading card inside!

and

The Honest-to-goodness Switcheroo

by G. M. Berrow

Coming Soon!

Turn the page for a
Special Surprise from
Rarity!

Dear reader,

I threw together these dazzling bonus pages just for you! Have fun glamming them up and sharing them with your fabulous friends!

Your favorite fashionista,
Rarity

RARITY'S GOWN MELTDOWN

Rarity has to design a dress to wear for the Ponyville Days Festival, but she is totally stuck! Sometimes, all it takes is a little help from a friend to be inspired. Can you help her by putting your own design on this pony dress form? Make it fabulous!

VERY PRETTY KITTY

Opalescence is Rarity's perfect sewing companion. She is always there to lend a fuzzy ear for listening (or scratching)! Do you have a pet? Use the space below to draw a picture of your pet. If you don't have one, draw the pet you would like to have. Don't forget to give it a spectacular name!

Pet Name: _____

Animal Type: _____

Favorite Treats: _____

SEARCHING FOR SAPPHIRES

The Pony of Pop—Sapphire Shores—has asked Rarity to sew her a new costume for the Equestria Music Awards! Rarity has been hard at work sewing but has come up short in her gem supply. She needs at least ten more sapphires to complete the outfit. Can you help her? Circle the sapphires below!

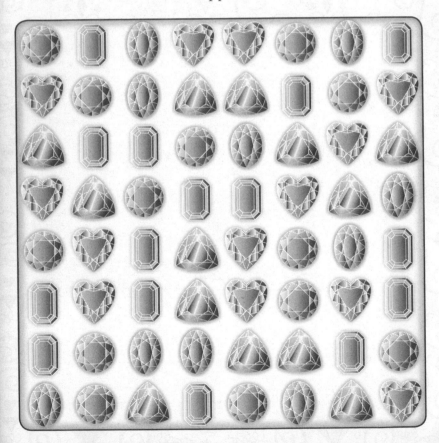

sapphire

diamond

amethyst

ruby

emerald

Pampered Ponies

Whenever Rarity wants to unwind from a long day at the Carousel Boutique, she visits the Ponyville Day Spa, where her friends offer relaxing beauty treatments. There are so many to choose from! Help Rarity decide by circling your choice for each category.

Mane Style:
straight   curly   updo

Hooficure Polish Color:
purple   silver   green   clear

Face Mask Type:
mud   avocado   honey

Spa Bubble Scent:
lavender   rose   chocolate

I look divine, thanks to you, darling!

WHAT'S iN A NAME?

*Names often have other meanings. For example,
Charity is proud that her name means generosity.
Rarity, on the other hoof, means special or unique.
Does your name have another meaning?
What about your family members or friends?
If you need help, try asking an adult to look it up
with you in a book or online.*

Name	Meaning
Rarity	a person or thing that is special, unique

Speak "Chic and Magnifique!"

Learning a foreign language can be lots of fun!
Just ask Rarity—some of her favorite phrases
are French. They just sound so classy, non?
Match the phrases with their English meanings.
Soon you'll sound just like Rarity!

très chic
(Hint: A pony has to be this to be considered a fashionista!)

_____

au revoir
(Hint: You should say this when you are leaving your favorite boutique.)

_____

haute couture
(Hint: Only the fanciest stores stock this type of clothing.)

_____

voilà
(Hint: You can say this when you're finished with a project.)

_____

HIGH FASHION   •   VERY STYLISH

LOOK HERE   •   GOOD-BYE

SHOPPING LIST SCRAMBLE

Rarity is very specific with her orders—she's definitely a pony who knows what she wants. Charity wants to get everything perfect for her mentor. Help her sort out this shopping list by unscrambling the words below.

1. VLEVTE

_ _ _ _ _ _

2. SNITA

_ _ _ _ _

3. NIBBRO

_ _ _ _ _ _

4. MEG

_ _ _

5. DRETAH

_ _ _ _ _ _

6. LEEEDN

_ _ _ _ _ _

PONYVILLE POST MIX-UP

The mail pony has some letters to deliver, but she's
a little bit confused! She needs your help to make
sure the right packages get to the right ponies.
Draw a line from each package to its pony owner.

CHARITY'S TRAVEL LOG

Rarity's apprentice, Charity, loves visiting new places! Before spending time in Ponyville, she lived in Mare-is, Prance, studying haute couture. Use the space below to keep track of the fun places you've been. The library, the zoo, and even camping in the backyard count, too!

Location	When Did You Visit?	Favorite Part of Trip
Crystal Empire	Summer	Seeing the Crystal Heart!

THE FOAL FREE PRESS CROSSWORD

Everypony needs to have a break now and then. One of Rarity's favorite things to do while she sips her tea is read THE FOAL FREE PRESS *newspaper. The crossword section is tons of fun! Help Rarity with this week's puzzle.*

ACROSS:

3. A little dragon with a big crush

5. Ponyville's prettiest fashionista kitty (for short)

7. A talented young apprentice with a lot to give and a lot to learn

8. A pony's beautiful hair

DOWN:

1. A stylish pony who has a beautiful heart and is known throughout Equestria for her designs

2. The most prestigious fashion society in Equestria

3. A sweet little sister

4. Rarity's true passion—other than friendship!

6. Rarity's favorite piece of clothing to sew for her friends

DESIGN A MARE ÉCLAIR

Rarity and Charity have so much in common, including their favorite fashion magazine, Mare Éclair. If you could design a magazine, what would you put on the cover? Write your own ideas for cool features in this issue of Mare Éclair!

MARE ÉCLAIR

Beauty and Style